Groovy Girls

Sleepover Club

Girls of Summer

Bon Voyage

Robin Epstein

Scholastic Inc.

New York   Toronto   London   Auckland   Sydney
Mexico City   New Delhi   Hong Kong   Buenos Aires

Read all the books about the Groovy Girls!

#1 The First Pajama Party

#2 Pranks a Lot

#3 Sleepover Surprise

#4 Rock and Roll

#5 Choose or Lose

#6 The Great Outdoors

#7 Growing Up Groovy

#8 Girls of Summer

In memory of Jane Love,
an inspiration to all girls, no matter how old

Cover illustration by Taia Morley

Interior illustrations by Yancey Labat

ISBN 0-439-81438-3

© 2005 Manhattan Group, LLC
All rights reserved. Published by Scholastic Inc.
SCHOLASTIC, LITTLE APPLE, and associated logos are trademarks and/or
registered trademarks of Scholastic Inc.

The Groovy Girls™ books are produced under license from Manhattan Group, LLC.
Go to groovygirls.com for more Groovy Girls fun!

12 11 10 9 8 7 6 5 4 3 2 1   5 6 7 8 9 10/0
Printed in the U.S.A.
First Little Apple printing, September 2005

CHAPTER 1
Summertime, Summertime,
Sum-Sum-Summertime 1

CHAPTER 2
A Sleepover Send-Off 9

CHAPTER 3
You Got Bunk'd! 15

CHAPTER 4
The *Chi-Chi* City 23

CHAPTER 5
Good to Go! 33

CHAPTER 6
Mail Call 43

CHAPTER 7
The End?!? 51

CHAPTER 8
Or the Beginning? 59

PLUS
Sleepover Handbook 8

Summertime, Summertime, Sum-Sum-Summertime

"T he End!" O'Ryan yelled happily, as she and the Groovies left school that afternoon. "The end, the end, theeeee ennnnnd!"

"It's all over but the shouting!" Gwen responded, yelling out the window of the school bus on the girls' ride home. "THE! END!"

And since the very last hour of the very last day

of the school year had come and gone, the Groovy Girls were now the See Ya Later, School Girls!

"I mean, I'm happy school's over, but even better than that—" O'Ryan exclaimed, grabbing her best friend, Oki, by the arm, "that means SUMMER'S STARTING! Aren't you excited? Isn't it the greatest that we're going to soccer camp together?"

"Uh-huh," Oki replied, a little too quickly.

"Beyond great!" O'Ryan continued, drumming on her thigh. "It's greaty-great-GREAT!"

"And the Camp Mohawk website sure does make it look supreme," Reese added. "I mean, those log cabin bunks look *Little-House-on-the-Prairie* amazing and it's going to be so much fun to share a bunk bed with my best friend, Gwen!"

"I know," Gwen said. "With me, you, O'Ryan, and Oki going, it'll be like a week-long Groovy Girl slumber party, minus Vanessa and Yvette, of course."

"So that'd make it a G-R-O-O, GROO party," Vanessa replied.

"And Vanessa and I will

be having a very V-Y, VY party of our own at Camp All Stars," Yvette said, smiling at her best friend.

Whereas Camp Mohawk specialized in sports, Camp All Stars had programs in drama (a perfect fit for a superstar-to-be singer like Yvette) and debate (which was ideal for Vanessa).

"Well, I hope you guys have fun there," O'Ryan said to Yvette and Vanessa, "'cause I know Camp Mohawk is going to be great for me and Oki. I mean, it's like a combo of everything I like best in the world. I get to be with my best friend, plus my best sister, and my best sister's best friend, and I get to play sports. If there's any homework, it'll be stuff I love doing—like practicing my head-butting skills—and—"

"I don't think you need any more practice butting heads," Reese said, teasing her seven-minutes-older twin. "You're already pretty good at doing that with Mom when she tells you to clean up your side of our room!"

"You can joke all you want," O'Ryan replied, "but I'm way too excited to even *bother* reminding you that I was MVP of my soccer team this year."

"Co-MVP," Reese corrected. "I believe your team captain—or should I say your lover boy—Mike, was also given the MVP award."

At the mention of Mike's name—okay, at the mention of the words "lover boy," too—O'Ryan's face turned a bright red.

"Mike is *not* my lover boy!" O'Ryan replied, lowering her voice at the words "lover boy," and trying hard not to let her twin's teasing interfere with her happy mood. "Besides," O'Ryan added, hurriedly changing the subject, "school is over! Camp is starting! And I just feel like dancing!"

And so, despite the no-dancing-in-the-aisles-when-the-bus-is-in-motion rule, that's exactly what O'Ryan started to do.

But when Oki, O'Ryan's best pal and dance partner, didn't get up to join her, O'Ryan gave a sideways glance in her best friend's direction.

"Hey, Oki, what's the deal? Aren't you as excited as I am that the two of us are going to RULE that camp?"

"Well..." Oki said, looking down at her shoes.

"Well, what?" O'Ryan replied, stopping her dance as Oki's bus stop approached. "What's wrong?"

"Nothing's wrong, exactly," Oki answered.

"Well, you don't seem nearly as jazzed about camp as I do. I mean, don't you think we're all going to have the *best* time together?"

"Yes, I mean, I'm sure everyone will have an amazing time!" Oki replied, as she picked up her backpack from the floor and curled the straps over her shoulders.

"Oki," Reese responded, tilting her head to the side, "you make it sound like you're not going with us."

"Well, that's the thing," Oki replied. "See, I've been meaning to tell you—actually, I just found out—I'm not."

SCREEEEEEECH!!! went the sound track in O'Ryan's head.

"*What?!*" O'Ryan shouted. "What do you mean you're not going?"

"I can't," Oki said, taking a big deep breath.

"Of course you can," O'Ryan replied. "We've had it planned for ever 'n' ever!"

"Yeah, I know," Oki said. "But the thing is, my

mom just found out she's going on a business trip to Paris that week, and she thought it would be fun to make a family vacation out of it...I didn't quite know how to tell you."

"So you're going to Paris instead?" Gwen asked, her eyes getting wide.

"Uh-huh," Oki said.

"You're going to *Paris*?" O'Ryan repeated. "When, exactly?"

Oki shrugged. "The trip is the same week as camp, so that's why I can't go."

"Wow!" Reese said as Oki stood up, preparing to get off the bus. "How exciting!"

"I know. I'm still kind of in shock about it!" Oki replied. "I've always-always-always wanted to go to Paris—ever since I was a little girl! It really is a dream come true!"

"But that means you won't be coming to camp?" O'Ryan asked, as if she still could not quite believe that her best friend wouldn't be by her side.

"Right," Oki replied. "Ooh, okay, this is me. I gotta go, guys," she added when the bus came to a halt at her stop. And with that, Oki blew her friends kisses and skipped off the bus. *"Au revoir,"* she said, over her shoulder. "See you at the slumber party tonight!"

"That's the grooviest," Yvette said when the bus started rolling again.

"Yeah, how fun for her," Vanessa agreed.

But all O'Ryan could continue to say was, "She's not going to camp with us?"

So, even though it was the last day of school—the best day of the whole entire year next to your birthday, Halloween, and Christmas—all the thrill, all the excitement, and all the joy just seemed to seep right out of O'Ryan, like a balloon that had just been pierced with a pin. And she was left to wonder: How, with the mention of just one tiny little word—*Paris*—could she have gone from elated to deflated so quickly?

Chapter 2

A Sleepover Send-Off

"Oki," Yvette said, as the girls stood in the McCloud's kitchen that slumber-party Friday night, "in honor of your trip to Paris, I think we should make Parisian pizzas!"

"That's a great idea," Vanessa agreed. "And we should make them with baguettes."

"What's that?" asked Gwen. "A new kind of bologna?"

"Nooo." Vanessa giggled. "Bag-*ettes* are what the French call their long, skinny loaves of bread."

"That's right," confirmed Oki, "and they buy them in bread shops. It's all terribly chic!"

Oki was looking pretty chic herself. And just to be sure she didn't add any "decorations" to her outfit with ingredients for the pizza, she put on an apron.

While Yvette, Vanessa, and Oki got busy with the pizza prep, Reese and Gwen folded camp socks into little balls at the kitchen table. After all, the girls were leaving for Camp Mohawk on Monday, and they needed to get cracking with their packing.

"I think I'm one sock short," Reese said, holding up a spare sock.

"Well, just turn one sock inside out and then *wallah!* You get a whole second wearing out of it," Gwen replied.

"Smashingly smart!" Reese answered.

But instead of packing her clothes or participating in the French bread pizza party for Oki, O'Ryan was just moping.

"A little help with spreading the pizza sauce," said Yvette, turning to Vanessa.

"Hey, do any of you chefs need us to pitch in?" asked Reese.

"Nah, I think we've got the job *covered*," replied Vanessa as she spread a layer of the red sauce over one slice of French bread.

"*Ooh-la-la*, O'Ryan, pass me the *fromage*, please," Oki said, holding up the cheese grater.

"The *what*?" O'Ryan said, sort of understanding, but not feeling in the mood to play along.

"You know," Oki replied, "pass the cheese, please."

"It's in the fridge," O'Ryan responded, making no move to get it and heading to the living room instead.

"O'Ryan," Oki said, putting the grater down and following her best friend out of the kitchen. "Are you okay?"

"Am I okay?" O'Ryan replied, throwing herself into a beanbag chair. "No, I'm not okay! In fact, I'm supremely heartsick right now." O'Ryan patted her chest, as if to show

exactly where she was feeling it, too.

"But you've been over-the-moon excited for camp."

"Yeah," O'Ryan said, sitting up, "but that's when I thought we'd be going over the moon together. I mean, I didn't know I was going to have to go there best-friendless."

"O'Ryan," Oki said, squishing herself into the beanbag beside her friend. "You won't be best-friendless! It's just that we'll both be on separate vacations. And yours is going to be just as amazingly incredible as mine."

"Well, it *would* have been amazingly incredible," O'Ryan replied, pulling away from Oki and standing up. "I mean, it's sports camp—one whole week of the things I like best in the world—but without you there with me, I just don't know how it's going to be any fun."

"I'll e-mail you every single day," Oki said.

"But you don't even speak French—I mean, I know you know a couple of words and stuff," O'Ryan said, frowning, "so how will you be able to work the keyboard?"

"O'Ryan, it's not like the French speak Russian! They use exactly the same alphabet we do, so the keyboards are almost the same," Oki replied.

"Well, you'll probably be too busy climbing to the top of the Eiffel Tower or something to even *think* about me."

There were a lot of things Oki wanted to do in Paris! It was one of the pizzaz-ziest cities in the world, after all, and she knew she'd be one busy bee in Par-ee. But no way would she forget about her best friend while she was there!

"O'Ryan," Oki said, getting up from the beanbag and bopping her friend on the shoulder with a pillow. "I'll e-mail you as often as I can, I promise. Plus," Oki added with a smile, "think of what a huge star you're going to be at camp! Everyone's gonna know you're the best soccer player around—I mean, especially 'cause you won't have me there stealing your thunder on the field!"

This made O'Ryan laugh. Though Oki had always been an "enthusiastic" soccer player, a great player she was not. (And she was the first one to admit it!)

O'Ryan looked at her best friend, and they hugged. How could anyone ever stay mad at Oki?

"So should we go back into the kitchen and help out with the *Bon Voyage* Baguettes?" O'Ryan asked Oki.

"*Oui, oui!*" Oki nodded.

And with that, the best friends walked back into the kitchen, where they proceeded to have a "grate" time chopping up cheese and placing mushrooms, tomatoes, and red peppers on top of their homemade, very French bread pizzas!

Chapter 3

You Got Bunk'd!

WELCOME TO CAMP MOHAWK

"Top or bottom? Bottom or top?"

These were the questions Gwen kept repeating to Reese as they arrived at camp Monday around noon. The girls wanted to claim their bunk space ASAP to be sure they'd get to share a bunk bed, something they'd only been talking about doing for, like, forever.

"Bottom," Reese finally said when the girls entered their cabin, throwing her duffel bag onto the lower bunk of the beds by the windows. "Definitely bottom for me."

"*Terrif*, then I'll take top and you can smell my sweet feet!" Gwen responded with a giggle, and scrambled up the ladder to the top bed.

"Um, *hello*?" said O'Ryan, when she walked into the bunk.

Unlike Gwen and Reese, O'Ryan had taken some time to look around the grounds before heading to their cabin. Until now, she'd been more interested in checking out the fields where she'd be playing soccer than worrying about beds 'n' stuff.

But when O'Ryan saw that Gwen was plopping her stuff down on the top bunk—*her* bed!—her eyes widened. "That's where *I'm* supposed to sleep!" O'Ryan said.

"Really?" Gwen asked, looking confused and hanging her head over the bed to glance down at Reese. "But Reese and I have been talking about sharing a bunk bed since before school ended. I mean, we're BFFs, after all."

"Well, yeah," O'Ryan said, "but Reese is my sister, so..."

So this put Reese in a rather uncomfortable position. She was being asked to choose between her best friend and her twin, and that stunk...stunk worse than Gwen's "sweet" feet.

Reese knew that if Oki had been at camp with them, this wouldn't have been an issue. But Oki *wasn't* there, of course, and Reese wanted to be sensitive to her twin's sitch.

But what could she do? Would she really have to tell her best friend that she had to break the bunk-bed-sharing-pinkie-promise they'd made?

Was that fair?

Nope, didn't think so!

"O'Ryan," Reese said as kindly as she could, "the thing is, we sleep in the same room together every night when we're at home. So this is kind of a special thing for Gwen and me. You can understand that, right?"

O'Ryan didn't respond with words, she just shook her head "no" from side to side.

But, of course, O'Ryan *could* understand it. In fact, she understood it very well because she'd been equally excited by the idea of getting to share a bunk bed with Oki. But at that very moment, Oki was on a plane to Paris! And even though Oki had reassured O'Ryan that she'd have fun at Camp Mohawk without her, O'Ryan was already beginning to feel like the odd girl out.

"Fine!" O'Ryan said eventually, not really thinking it was fine at all.

As she looked around the room in search of a new place, another girl pointed to her bunk and asked O'Ryan if she wanted the top bed.

"Um, yeah, I guess. Thanks," O'Ryan replied, looking at the girl. She seemed nice enough, after all.

In fact, everyone that O'Ryan had met so far seemed nice...but no one seemed nearly as groovy as Oki.

But just as O'Ryan was beginning to think about how much she was missing her best friend, the sound of a whistle blew from outside, and the girls heard: "Bunk Five campers, come on out and line up, please!"

"I think that means us." Gwen laughed, jumping off her bed with a thud. "Hey, wait a second, if we're in Bunk Five, that makes us the Bunk Five Beauties!" she added, making up a group nickname.

"Well, come on then," replied Reese, "let's act like beauties and mark the spot!"

So the girls hop-scotched outside and listened as their counselor, Suzanne, explained what they'd be doing that day: running, jumping, kicking, sliding, and just generally hot-dogging it all around the field. But first, they were going to start out with some skills tests.

"Well, I can tell you right now, my arms are pretty weak," said Gwen, "but my teeth are crazy strong!"

"It's true," Reese added. "Gwen can chew through a pizza box!"

"Keep it down," O'Ryan said, not wanting to miss a word about how their days would be organized. For her, soccer was no joking matter.

"Hey, I have a question," Reese said to their counselor, ignoring her sister. "What are we going to do when we're not playing soccer?" Reese was already looking forward to the time when she could do anything but.

"Well, there's always arts and crafts," Suzanne replied. "Because we want you to be well-rounded athletes."

"Speaking of well-rounded," Gwen replied, "when's lunch?"

"After the skills tests. So let's get started, shall we?" Suzanne blew her whistle, and all the girls took off for the soccer field.

O'Ryan was more than ready to let her pent-up energy start pouring out, and as soon as she got the signal, she tore down the field, dribbling a soccer ball through a crazy zigzag of orange traffic cones, far in front of any of her other bunk mates.

Whatever bunk-bed rage or best-friend absence she had been feeling, she was soon taking it out on that black-and-white soccer ball, which she kicked, flipped, and headed all around the field.

"Look at her go!" Reese said, amazed by the performance, which was good even for O'Ryan.

"She looks like a pinwheel!" Gwen added, crumpling at the waist when she could run no more.

As soon as the skills drills were over, O'Ryan jogged to the large orange jugs of water and splashed some on her face.

Suzanne was tallying the scores on everyone's tests, and when she looked at O'Ryan's numbers, her eyes widened. "You're quite the outstanding player, O'Ryan," Suzanne said.

Every camper in Bunk Five applauded O'Ryan and gave her high fives.

She was their new star!

"Oh, wow, thanks!" O'Ryan replied, trying not to sound too pleased with herself.

Now *this* was how O'Ryan imagined camp was supposed to be. Finally, at long last, things seemed to be looking up. Until Suzanne walked over and said:

"Of course, this means we've got a problem."

"A problem?" O'Ryan asked.

What could be the problem? The fact that she was much better than everyone else, as Suzanne went on to explain to her, didn't exactly seem like it should be a problem...until O'Ryan looked at the rest of her bunk mates and realized they had all already been paired up according to their skill level.

Oh, no!

"Maybe I could play with some of the bigger girls," O'Ryan suggested, glancing down the field to where some of the other bunks were practicing.

"No good, they're all out of your age group," Suzanne replied, pulling on the bill of her baseball cap. "But don't you worry, we'll find you someone."

O'Ryan nodded, then booted the ball as far as she could, clear down the field. She didn't even mean to send the ball hurtling so far away—but her kick was so strong, she couldn't help it.

"I'll just go get that," O'Ryan said, slightly embarrassed by the power in her legs. But as she ran for the ball, O'Ryan thought that, though it might be slightly lonely at the top, there was something pretty special about being in a class all by herself!

Chapter 4
The Chi-Chi City

"Oh-la-la," said Oki, stepping off the jet Tuesday morning in Paris.

Oki's ooh-la-la-ing actually had less to do with her first impression of Paris than with her head-spinning tiredness—a combination of jet lag and the seven-hour time difference between Paris and home.

Still, as soon as Oki walked into the terminal and saw all the signs written in French, heard airport announcements spoken in that glorious la-dee-da language and watched all the other travelers hustling by, she got a second wind.

"Wowee!" Oki said, skipping down the long corridors of the airport. "Are we really here? Are we really in Paris, France?!" Oki could barely believe it, and she started spinning around in perfect pirouettes.

After they picked up their luggage (or "les bagages," as the French say), Oki and her mother hopped in a taxi, (or "un taxi," as the French say) and headed straight for their hotel (yep, you guessed it, a "hôtel," as the French say) in the center of the city.

"Hey, wait a second!" Oki said, her nose pressed against the taxi window as she watched the city glide by. "I think it's starting to rain!"

She turned to her mom as if to get a second opinion because this just didn't seem right. Oki had never imagined that it would rain in Paris. Whenever she pictured the city, the sun was always shining, the flowers were in bloom, and the fashionable streets glittered brightly!

And as the raindrops started pelting against the taxi window, Oki's smile began to dim. *Rain, rain, go away!* she thought to herself. But just then, "le taxi" drove right past L'Arc de Triomphe, a magnificent gateway arch.

"WHOOOOAAAAA!" Oki yelled. "Paris is even more beautiful than I've been picturing. And you know what else, Mom?" she said excitedly, without turning away from the view. "The rain won't be a major biggie because we'll be spending all day in the shops and museums anyway, right?" Oki giggled with delight and kept talking. "This is just a dream come true!" she said, imagining herself at the top of the Eiffel Tower, and picturing herself examining art at the Louvre, the world-famous art museum. Come to think of it, this was even more vivid than a dream!

When they finally got to their hotel, Oki hung up her clothes in the big closet armoire—after all, she wanted to be as wrinkle-free as possible in France—and then looked expectantly at her mother. But her mother was neither hanging clothes, nor preparing to hit the town. Instead, she was simply getting ready for a nap.

"Um...okay, are you ready to go?" Oki asked,

as she started bouncing on her mom's bed. "MAAHHHMMM, come on! We're in France. We can sleep when we get back to the good old U.S. of A.!"

Well, Oki *did* make a good argument—and the fact that she kept bouncing on the bed, making it impossible for her mother to sleep, made the decision even easier.

"Okay, okay, put on your best Parisian poncho, and let's explore the city!" her mother finally replied.

Oki didn't need to hear it twice. She danced around the hotel room and selected an outfit she was sure would wow the Frenchies she passed in the street.

And hot-diggity! When she looked at herself in the mirror after dressing—putting on purple polka-dotted tights, a matching scarf, and pink knee-high boots—the fabulous girl staring back at her looked like she'd spent all her summers in France.

Though they'd certainly planned to get to all the cultural hot spots in Paris, Oki convinced her mother it might be best to start off with something a little more familiar to both of them: SHOPPING!

And as Oki rolled through the revolving doors of the giant French department store, Les Galeries Lafayette, looking, she thought, very Parisian indeed, she couldn't help but wonder if people would mistake her for a native and start speaking to her in French!

But she soon stopped thinking about herself, since the store itself was so incredible—the clothes, handbags, jewelry, and multi-colored-designer shoes extended as far as the eye could see!

Oki ran her hand against the smooth leather of the handbags. She began trying on all the hats she could reach. And by the time she got to the girls' department, she was virtually floating on air.

"Oh my, oh my, oh my!" Oki exclaimed when she saw a skirt adorned with peacock feathers. "I must have this! No. Wait. This!" she said, rubbing her face against a silky champagne-colored camisole. *"Attend, attend, attend!"* she said, repeating the French word for "wait, wait, wait!"

Her mother waited.

"Well," said Oki, "since this really *is* such a special trip, Mom, what do you say to buying a whole bunch of things, so we can have lots of reminders of our amazing time in Paris when we get back? And since I'm going to be a fashion designer when I grow up, it'll be, like, homework."

When her mother tilted her head to the side, Oki had a pretty good idea what she was about to say: *Uh...no.*

"Oki," her mother replied, "choose your *one* favorite thing, and we can use that as a reminder, okay?"

Oki's mouth dropped open.

"ONE thing?" she asked in disbelief. "How am I *ever* going to be able to choose just one thing from this groov-alicious department store of all things chic and vogue-y?"

"Good question," her mother replied. "I guess you're going to have to make your selection very wisely. So I'll be sitting over in that big chair preparing for my big meeting tomorrow while you decide."

Oh, the injustice!

Oh, the wrongness!

Oh, how Oki wished O'Ryan were there so she could share her feelings of unfairness, upset, and confusion!

But then, remembering that her mother had brought her to Paris, and that this, in and of itself, was a very generous gift, Oki nodded. "Okay," she said, "you just sit down there and when I find the most outrageously stylie and fantastically Frenchy piece of clothing I can find, I'll bring it over to you."

Oki went to work sorting through tank tops and Capri pants, mini-skirts, micro-minis, scoop-necks, turtlenecks, three-quarter-length shirts, skorts, and jeans. She was awash in leather and denim, satin, corduroy, and fur. She touched silk, swept against cashmere, and ultimately pulled out one gorgeous, fuzzy sweater that she just adored.

"Mom! Mom!" Oki finally shouted with glee. "I found IT!"

But instead of sharing her moment of joy, Oki saw that her mother was having a conversation with another woman.

"Eva, meet Oki," Oki's mom said when Oki skipped over. "Oki, meet Eva."

"*Bonjour*, Oki, it is veh-ry nice to meet you," Eva said in a heavy French accent.

"*Bonjour*," Oki replied, with a slight curtsy. (After all, she was in France, and she wanted to give a proper French hello.)

"I was just telling your *maman*," Eva continued, "that I am the editor of a fashion journal here in Paris. It is called, *La Vie*. Have you heard of it?"

Oki nodded her head, *yes, of course*!

Of course, she'd NEVER heard of this paper before, but there was no way she was going to admit that to this real-live Frenchwoman.

"When I saw you searching through the clothes," Madame Eva continued, "I knew *immédiatement* that I wanted to feature you in a story we are doing for my paper."

Oki's eyes widened, and she realized she couldn't speak.

"So what do you say, Oki?" Madame Eva continued. "Would you model in a photo shoot for us?"

This was a question Oki had been waiting to hear every single day of her nine years of life (though she didn't realize that until now!).

"*Would* I?" Oki replied, still having a hard time believing the question.

"Well," Madame Eva added, "I should tell you that you can keep *all* of the clothes you model in the fashion shoot. Does that make it sound even better to you?"

Oki nodded. In fact, her head began bobbing so uncontrollably in the "YES!!!" direction, she realized if she didn't stop, Madame Eva might think there was something wrong with her.

Get it under control, girl, Oki thought to herself. *Speak!*

"YES!!!" Oki finally exclaimed. "You bet!

Absolutely, for sure, no question about it." Then she added: "I mean, *OUI!*"

And so, Madame Eva gave Oki's mother her business card and asked her to call her office the next morning so they could arrange the details of the fashion shoot.

La Vie
Madame Eva
Fashion Editor

"Do you believe this?! Do you believe this?!," Oki kept asking, when Madame Eva left. "Not only am I going to be a model for all the girls in France, I get to bring home all the clothes my little heart desires, too!"

As she walked to the exit with her mom, Oki reflected on the amazing time she was having. *Paris is not only a place that I've dreamed of for years*, Oki thought to herself, *it's a place where all my dreams have come true!*

"*Foie gras!*" Oki giggled, all of the sudden remembering her best friend. "O'Ryan is NEVER going to believe this!"

Chapter 5
Good to Go!

"Okay, I'm ready to go," Gwen said softly, bright and early Tuesday morning, so softly she wasn't sure Reese had heard her.

"You're ready to go where?" asked Reese, waking up and rubbing the sleep out of her eyes. She hoped Gwen didn't mean she was ready to go on a nature hike or something. After all the running around the girls had done yesterday, Reese's legs were feeling crazy sore.

"Home," Gwen nodded.

Huh?

Reese looked up at Gwen. "What do you mean you're ready to go home? It's only the start of the second day of camp, Gwen!"

"Uh-huh, I know," Gwen replied quietly. "And I'm ready to go home."

Most of the other girls in Bunk Five were still asleep, but Gwen was already dressed and had even packed her trunk.

"Gwen, how long have you been up?" Reese asked in a whisper.

"For a while," Gwen replied, shrugging her shoulders. "Well, kinda since last night, actually. I really don't think I slept much, since I was too scared about rolling off the bed and falling to the floor."

"Oh, Gwen, that's miserable! No wonder you're all discombobulated," Reese said, climbing up the ladder to sit by her friend. "So you know what? Let's trade beds, and then you'll start feeling better about things."

"Um, no, that's okay. I just want to go home."

"Rise and shine, Bunk Five Beauties!" yelled Counselor Suzanne, flinging open the bunk door and letting the bright sunlight flood the cabin.

Reese looked at Gwen, hoping Suzanne's usage of Gwen's bunk nickname would make her friend smile *a little*...but no such luck.

"Time to wash up so we can get good and dirty out on those fields today!" Suzanne continued. "So let's hustle and get up and get going to breakfast."

"Yeah, come on, Gwen," Reese said, getting dressed, "I think I even saw that they're going to be serving waffles. You *love* waffles!"

But when Gwen carefully climbed down from her bed, she just shook her head. "Not hungry, thanks."

"You're not?!" Reese asked.

Impossible! What was this...upside-down day?

Reese had never known Gwen as a girl who either:

1. didn't want to participate in activities, or

2. didn't want to participate in breakfast.

"Are you sick?" Reese asked, thinking that could be the only explanation for Gwen's odd behavior.

"No, I'm not sick, I just—" Gwen said, but then stopped.

She wasn't feeling sick, exactly...but she knew she wasn't feeling like herself, either.

In fact, just at that moment, Gwen felt a tear start sliding down her cheek.

"I just want to call my mom and have her come get me," Gwen said.

"Oh, Gwen!" Reese responded, pulling her friend into a warm hug. "Well, look, the fun hasn't even really started yet, you know? I think we're supposed to be having a tug-of-war this afternoon and then scrimmaging against the boys in Bunk Six. And if you went home now, you'd miss all that!"

"Yes, but if I went home," Gwen replied, wiping the wet from her cheeks, "I'd get to sleep in my own bed, under the glow-in-the-dark stars I stuck to my ceiling. And if I just wanted to sit down and chill out for a little while, I could curl up in my best comfy chair and watch some TV."

The comforts of home *did* sound nice, but Reese was pretty sure that if Gwen "chilled" at camp for a little while longer, she'd start having a great time there, too.

"C'mere," Reese said to Gwen, sitting her down on the lower bunk. "Look, let's think about this for a minute. I mean you, me, and Reese, we're all here together, and Vanessa and Yvette are off at Camp All Stars, probably having a fantastic time. And Oki's bopping around Paris. So if you went home now, none of us would be there to hang out with you. But, here's what I'm thinking: Let's you and me go to breakfast now, and if you still feel like you want to call your mom to pick you up afterward, we'll *both* go and find you a phone to use, okay?"

"Okay," Gwen said, realizing that, whether she was going or staying, she *still* had to have breakfast.

And just knowing her best friend was there for her *did* make Gwen feel a little better, so the two girls walked out of their cabin and headed for the mess hall.

O'Ryan, meanwhile, had headed off to breakfast already. She couldn't wait for the start of the real activities—all the skills tests yesterday had merely whetted her appetite for the beginning of game play today! And as she was carrying her tray full of waffles from the line to the Bunk Five table, she felt a tap on the shoulder.

"Hey there, O'Ryan," Suzanne said. "I was just chatting with one of the other counselors about you. And I think we've found your match."

"You were?" O'Ryan asked. "You did?"

"Yup. I was saying that I had a real rocket of a soccer player in my bunk, and I needed to find a hotshot to challenge you. So put down your tray for a sec and come outside with me."

"Wow!" O'Ryan replied. The thought of being challenged to her utmost potential was *exactly* why she'd come to camp. This was the greatest. Perfect!

"O'Ryan, meet your new partner!" Suzanne said as they reached the field and stopped in front of a male counselor, who was standing next to...

MIKE?!?!

"Wait," O'Ryan said, confused. "Where is she?"

"Right here in front of you!" Suzanne replied. "But I wouldn't call 'him' a 'her' if I were you!"

"Mike?" O'Ryan said, refusing to believe that he was actually who Suzanne had meant. "You mean, you want *Mike* to be my practice buddy?"

There was no way on earth Suzanne could possibly be suggesting something *that* crazy.

Impossible! What was this...upside-down day?

"You got it!" Suzanne nodded.

"But—" O'Ryan said, as she turned a bright shade of pink and let the rest of her sentence go unfinished—the part of the sentence where she would have said but couldn't, *"But Mike is a boy! But Mike is my next-door neighbor! But Mike is a guy I've pulled pranks on, and who's pulled them on me! But Mike is a guy I've always had a little crush on, and it would be unbelievably embarrassing to get paired up with him like this!"*

For his part, Mike didn't look too psyched about the news, either, and started turning a purply-mauve!

O'Ryan immediately thought that what she was thinking was probably pretty much what he was thinking, too.

She knew Mike thought she was a good

player—they had been co-MVPs on their co-ed school soccer team after all, which meant she was better than the rest of the boys. But she also knew that if they were paired, that he'd get mocked by the other boys even more than she'd get teased by the girls! And she was sure everyone would have a real "field day" when news of their pairing got around.

It'd be like a giant tease-a-palooza!

And now they were going to be in the middle of this "T" storm together.

"Hey, O'Ryan," Mike finally said, rolling his eyes and already imagining the teasing to come.

"Hi, Mike," O'Ryan replied, realizing they were both going to have to make the best of it.

"Great!" Suzanne said. "I knew this was going to work out wonderfully. So you guys go eat your breakfasts so you can be ready to get on the field in, like, twenty minutes, okay?"

O'Ryan and Mike both nodded.

"Holy cowbells," O'Ryan said as she steered over to the Bunk Five table.

Mike?

Mike!

Mike.

She put her tray down next to Reese and Gwen

and sat down, rubbing her hands against her face.

"Did I just see you talking to your lover boy outside?" Reese asked, batting her eyelashes

O'Ryan started to laugh.

After all, sometimes that was all you could do in a situation like this! In fact, the more O'Ryan thought about it, the funnier it seemed. And suddenly she was sure that if Oki were here, her best friend in all the world would be laughing along with her, just as loudly.

Chapter 6

Mail Call

From: Yvette <GirlSinger>
Sent: Wednesday, July 5, 6:24 PM
To: Vanessa <GirlDebater>
Subject: Where've Ya Been?

Vanessa!

Where are you??? Can't believe it's already Wednesday and we haven't seen each other once since we got here. Who knew they'd keep our programs so separate? I mean, for all I know, you debaters could have gone to Paris or somewhere...

Write back and let me know that you're still in the country!

XOXO
Yvette

From: Vanessa <GirlDebater>
Sent: Wednesday, July 5, 7:24 PM
To: Yvette <GirlSinger>
Subject: Right Here!

Hey, my singing super-star!

Wish I could tell you I *was* in Paris, but I'm still here on the other side of Camp All Stars (but speaking of France, wonder how *Mademoiselle* Oki is doing?).

Things over here are going okay, I guess...but just between you and me, it's turning out to be a lot harder than I was expecting. What's the 4-1-1 on your program?

Big Kiss,
Vanessa

From: Yvette <GirlSinger>
Sent: Wednesday, July 5, 7:45 PM
To: Vanessa <GirlDebater>
Subject: Mind Meld!

Things aren't exactly what I was

expecting here, either. Okay, like, on Monday, they held auditions for a musical that we're putting on at the end of the week called—believe it or not—"A Tree Falls in the Woods." Everyone was really nervous about the auditions. Well, I admit I wasn't really all that nervous (although maybe I should have been!). I mean, it's not like I'm bragging, but after how well I did in our school talent show, I *was* feeling pretty confident. But as soon as the first girl got up and started singing, I couldn't believe it! She was supreme. Then the next girl got up— and she was even better. The third girl? She was even better than the second! You get the idea. Turns out, most of these girls have taken professional singing lessons. PROFESSIONAL singing lessons! How am I supposed to compete with that?

X,
Yvette

Yvettester,

I totally know what you mean!!! Okay, so it's not exactly like the kids in my program are professional lawyers, but folks here are, like, scary smart! When they broke us into groups and told us we were going to give speeches on topics they were assigning, I didn't bother preparing. I mean, my topic was: *"Everybody loves peanut butter!"*

Well, I figured I could just kind of talk about it off the top of my head and be convincing, ya know? I mean, whenever we talk about stuff like that at our sleepovers, it's not like I ever do any research before blabbing. And all the Groovies usually end up listening to what I say! But when this other debater at camp got up there and gave the opposing point of view—*"Everybody loves jelly!"*—she had all these facts and figures at her fingertips. As you can imagine, I suddenly found myself in a real *sticky* situation!

Remember when they said at school that we're like "big fish in a little pond" 'cause we get a lot of attention and do pretty well? Well, here I'm feeling a lot more like a "little fish in a big pond" 'cause no matter what I say or do, it doesn't seem to make enough *waves*!

FROM: YVETTE <GIRLSINGER>
SENT: THURSDAY, JULY 6, 8:24 PM
TO: VANESSA <GIRLDEBATER>
SUBJECT: SOMETHING'S FISHY

Oh, V!

You'll always be a *whale* of a gal to me, but I soooo know what you mean! I'm feeling about as special here as tin foil. Get this: I didn't get the starring role of the woodpecker in "A Tree Falls in the Woods." Not even close. In fact, they put me in the chorus! I'm playing Pine Tree #3! How embarrassing is that? I mean, sure, there are lots of other girls with really pretty voices in the chorus, too. BUT STILL! I mean, who even *knew* pine trees could sing?

From: Vanessa <GirlDebater>
Sent: Thursday, July 6, 8:30 PM
To: Yvette <GirlSinger>
Subject: Oh, Say Can You Sing?

Well, seems to me like they must not know true talent when they see it if they only made you Pine Tree #3. I mean, I would have thought you'd at least have been made Pine Tree #1— just joking. But I'm sure you'll be the best tree in that forest!

As for me, I'm trying to work extra hard now so I can just keep my head *above water*. I mean, I can tell you this since you're my best friend in the whole world—and I know you won't tell anyone else—but when people voted on who gave the best speech, I came in dead last (and felt like the dumbest one in camp!).

You know what? No *way* could you be the dumbest one at camp! Even if everyone else there has the last name Einstein, I still wouldn't believe it! And as your best friend, it's my duty to remind you of how convincing you are as a leader at school and with the rest of the Groovies at our slumber parties and stuff. I mean, you even got me to believe that putting pepperoni and pineapple together on a pizza really tastes good!

You're still #1 in my book.

Aw, thanks! You just made me feel, like, a million times better. And I want to send exactly the same thoughts right back at you: you've always been an incredible performer and you always will be. Bottom line, Y, you're much more a "rock" star than a "pine tree" to me.

Oh, and here's something to make you smile: O'Ryan and Mike became partners at soccer camp! Gwen said she voted them "the cutest couple at camp." So at least *someone* we know is coming in first place at something!

XOX
V

FROM: YVETTE <GIRLSINGER>
SENT: THURSDAY, JULY 6, 8:55 PM
TO: VANESSA <GIRLDEBATER>
SUBJECT: AND THE (REAL) WINNER IS...

Too funny!

Anyway, V, you know what I think? That we should give ourselves a break. I mean, together we're the best singing tree and smoothest peanut butter debater this side of Camp All Stars! And how many best friends can say that?!

Much love, nighty-night, and see you soon,

Yvette

Chapter 7

The End?!?

"S CORE!!!

"NICE!" Mike said, running up to O'Ryan and high-fiving her for scoring the winning goal.

Big cheer from the crowd.

It was a great moment. It was, in fact, the perfect end to the final game of the final day at camp. Thanks to O'Ryan and Mike's "all star" teamwork, they'd brought home the win!

On their victory lap around the field, O'Ryan proudly said, "We crushed 'em!"

"You were The Crusher, all right," Mike replied with a laugh. "You don't play like a girl, that's for sure."

"Hey, you take that back!" O'Ryan said. "I do, *too*, play like a girl. Like an AMAZINGLY talented girl!"

"Yeah, okay, okay," Mike said, backing off and smiling as he bounced the soccer ball against his knee. "I guess I can't disagree with you there."

"So I suppose we'll keep playing together when we get home," O'Ryan replied.

Mike looked at O'Ryan and cocked his head. "Are you *kidding*?" he asked.

Suddenly, the color flared into O'Ryan's cheeks. OH, NO!

She'd stepped over the line! Made a foul play! Committed a major error!

Even though they were great practice partners here, life, of course, was going to return to normal when they got back home. How could O'Ryan have thought otherwise?

But then Mike said: "I mean, sure we're going to play together when we get back home." And then he added: "In fact, I think we're probably going to *have* to see even more of each other now!"

Now it was O'Ryan's turn to cock her head, and this time it was Mike's turn to blush furiously.

"Well," he added quickly, "what I mean is, if we want to keep in shape for the fall, we'll need to keep practicing, right?"

"Right!" O'Ryan said, smiling.

Riiiiiiight!

"I can't believe how much I learned," Vanessa said when she and Yvette had settled into the back seat of the bus that was bringing them home from Camp All Stars.

"So does that mean you liked camp or *didn't* like camp?" Yvette said, giggling.

"Hard to believe, but even though I had to do all that research stuff," V replied, "I have to say, I actually ending up enjoying it!"

"Wow," Yvette replied, "who knew you'd end up such a geek!" But when Vanessa's mouth dropped open, and she was about to protest, Yvette quickly added, "Just kidding!"

"Very funny, singing pine tree," Vanessa replied with a smile.

"Well, you're probably not going to believe this," Yvette responded, "but I actually came to *like* being in the chorus."

"Really?" Vanessa asked. "But I thought you were mad you didn't get to be lead woodpecker."

"Turns out, the big woodpecker wasn't all it was *pecked* up to be," Yvette said with a laugh. "The girl who got the part had to wear an ugly beak. And as a pine tree, at least I got to wear fir! Anyway, I bet next year I'll get an even *bigger* part, because after just one week at camp, I feel like I'm better already!"

"Ditto!" Vanessa replied. "My thoughts exactly."

"Excuse me!" Oki said to the flight attendant as the *chi-chi* lady came around to offer croissants and orange juice on the flight home. "Do you happen to have any copies of today's *La Vie*?"

The flight attendant smiled. "But of course!" she said in a lovely French accent. "I would have offered it to you sooner, but I did not realize you read French."

"Well," Oki smiled back, "I'm really more interested in the pictures. You see, I'm supposed to be featured in the fashion section that's running today!"

"Oh, *fantastique*!" the flight attendant replied, digging around her cart to find a copy of the paper. "Well, here you are, please let me know if you'd like me to help you translate any words that you don't understand."

"*Merci* you very much!" Oki said, excitedly tearing through the paper to find her picture.

Just imagine, me, Oki thought to herself, *a girl from Groovyland, U.S.A., turning out to be the model of style for French girls*!

And when she finally found herself in the center of the paper, Oki gasped.

The pictures were beautiful!

"Look, look, it's me!" she shouted.

And then she looked to the side to see if she could read the caption, and sure enough, she could!

"An American in Paris!" Oki read (since it was written in English). "An American in Paris???"

Wait a second!

She thought she was supposed to be a model for the French...but the only thing they took her as a model for was a typical American schoolgirl!

Oki clapped her hand over her mouth. She couldn't believe how backward she'd gotten it. But the more she thought about it, what difference did it make? She was still the toast of the town, even if she wasn't actually "French toast"!

•✿•

"I mean, I can't believe how much fun I had as soon as I stopped thinking about how much fun I usually have at home," Gwen said to Reese as the girls waited at the parking lot drop-off to be picked up.

"Well, what was your favorite part?" Reese asked.

"My favorite part? Ooh, toughie," Gwen replied. "Could have been the giant tug-of-war we had on Tuesday night against the boys in Bunk Six. Or it could have been when I scored my first goal ever on Wednesday. Or it could have been the giant Popsicle-stick castle I made. Or, it could have been just getting to be with you twenty-four/seven."

Reese smiled. "Yeah," she said, thinking about her own greatest moments. "I loved when we raided Bunk Six. And I had so much fun during color war, too. But my fave part could have been just getting to be with you twenty-four/seven, too!"

"I can't believe it," Gwen said suddenly.

"What?" Reese asked, confused.

"Look!"

The green car that was fast approaching was Gwen's mother!

"No, no, no, no, no, no, no!" Gwen exclaimed. "I'm not ready to go home! I don't want camp to end!"

Chapter 8

Or the Beginning?

"I may have bark but I don't have bite," Yvette sang, as she danced pine-tree style into the McCloud's living room for the first post-vacation Groovy Girls slumber party. "But beware my branches when you fly your kite!"

"*Voila!*" Oki exclaimed, digging five copies of *La Vie* out of her overnight bag and handing a copy to each Groovy Girl. "Check out the model on page fifteen. Is she cute or what?"

"Listen to this," Vanessa yelled, as she grabbed a slice of veggie supreme pizza and plunked herself down on the living room floor. "When I had to convince my audience that everyone loved peanut butter, I did the first half of my speech pretending like I had some stuck to the roof of my mouth!"

"Funny!" Gwen replied. "But get a load of this! Reese and I had a competition to see who could drink the most waffle syrup—and I won."

"Actually, I think we were *both* losers," Reese said.

"No wonder you guys were rolling around on the field that day!" O'Ryan replied, with a laugh.

"Oh, *yeah*? Well, how would you know?" Reese replied mischievously. "You were so busy making mooney-eyes at Mike, I didn't think you noticed!"

"Oh, I noticed all right," O'Ryan responded, without missing a beat. 'Cause a great soccer player knows how to keep her eye on the ball and still not miss a trick."

"*Touché!*" Oki said. "Great comeback!"

And speaking of comebacks, now that the Groovies had all *come back*, they happily began chatting about what they'd do together to make the rest of their sum-sum summertime utterly supreme and grandly groovy!

Groovy Girls™
sleepover handbook

How to Survive Vacation
Without Your Best Friend

JUICY POPS 8
&
Popsicle-Stick Picture Frames

Throw a Bon Voyage Sleepover

Funky Summer Shades

Contents

Bon Voyage Sleepover 4

Summer Survival Solutions 7

Sum-Sum-Summertime Fun 8

Dazzling Summer Duds 11

Popsicle Party 12

Popsicle-Stick Picture Frames........................... 13

French Baguette Pizza 14

Text by Suzanne Francis
Illustrations by Yancey Labat and Kurt Marquart

A Groovy Greeting

BONJOUR, GROOVY GIRL!

Summer's coming and we Groovies couldn't be more excited! We're so ready to pack up our bags and begin our sum-sum-summertime travels that we've been counting the days! *Un, deux, trois, quatre, cinq, six, sept, huit, neuf, dix.* You'll see why I'm counting in French in a sec. In the meantime, if you're ready for some vacation fun of your own, then read on!

Whether you're off to Paris like me, or to a week-long stay at camp like the rest of the Groovy Girls, get the gang together to say good-bye by throwing a *Bon Voyage* Sleepover! Pages 4-6 are chock-full of super ideas on how to send everyone off for the summer in style. *Magnifique!*

Summer is all about arts and crafts, right? You can make a Popsicle-stick picture frame (see page 13) to hold a photo of you and your friends, and use all the leftover sticks to make— what else—Popsicles, of course! See page 12 for all kinds of fun ones from Rainbow Pops to Creamy Orange. *Fantastique!*

If you're looking for even more ways to make summertime fun (*oui, oui!*), check out pages 8-10. With all the supreme suggestions, you'll wonder how to fit them all in! I think summer should definitely be longer! Don't you?

Well, you're on your way to a fabulous vacation for sure! Just remember, no matter where you go or what you do, stay groovy!

Au Revoir!
Oki

Bon Voyage Sleepover

Ready, like the Groovy Girls
in *Girls of Summer*, for vacation?
Throw a good-bye sleepover! You're
bound for great adventures whether you're
headed near or far, so get together and celebrate!

Traveling Denim Jacket

Choose a denim jacket (or a favorite comfy
sweatshirt) to share over the summer with
your friends. Pick names out of a hat to
figure out who gets the jacket first, and
agree on a time limit for the jacket's stay at
each stop. Promise to send the jacket to the
next girl on the list once you've had your turn.
Before sending it on its way, add a little something to it.
For example, you can glue a sparkling jewel onto a pocket,
stick a beaded pin on the collar, or paint a little heart on one
of the buttons. Or tuck a special note inside one of the pockets
to say "hi" or "wear me well" to the next girl who receives it!

Sleep on It

Turn plain old pillowcases
into dreamy gifts for your
friends to take with them
while they're away! Get a
bunch of fabric pens from
a craft store and give each
girl a pillowcase. Put a piece
of cardboard inside each

pillowcase (so that you have something to lean on while you decorate). Now get the creative vibes going! Use a pencil to sketch out what you want to draw or write

before taking pen to pillowcase. You can write messages like: "Have a Great Summer," "Think of Me," or "Sweet Dreams." You can draw pictures like stars and moons, or maybe sheep jumping over clouds! If you want everyone to sign your friend's pillowcase, send it around the circle and have each girl write a personal message to autograph it. That way, everyone can have all her friends on her mind while she sleeps!

Don't Open Till You're on Your Way

*Make a travel pack for your BFF to open once she's left for her trip. Include notes, magazine clippings, funny drawings, and games to play on the go. Once you have everything together, make a cool envelope to put it all in. Use wrapping paper, an old calendar, newspaper, or a road map. Place all your goodies in the center of the paper and cut the top half of the paper into a triangular shape. Then wrap it like you would a gift. Last, fold the triangular part over to make it look like a giant envelope.

*Or you can decorate a brown paper bag that you fill with goodies for your friend to take with her. Add your friend's favorite snack, a funny book to make her laugh, or that nail polish of yours that she loves. Cool gifts to go!

5

My Three

Ask everyone the question: "What three things can't you live without?" Whether you're headed to summer camp like O'Ryan, Reese and Gwen, or are Paris-bound like Oki, think about what things you'd take with you if you could only take three. Have each girl write down her choices on separate pieces of paper. Keep it a secret for now. Fold up the papers and put them into a bag. Pass the bag around and let each girl pick out a list. Take turns reading each list, and have everyone guess who wrote it.

Jar of the Future

You and your friends may be going your separate ways for the summer, but just think about all the things you'll have to catch up on—and do together— when everyone gets back! Make a "jar of the future" to make sure you don't miss out on anything. Get an old jar (such as a mayo or pickle jar) and wash it out. On separate slips of paper, each girl writes down the things she wants to do when everyone gets back. It can be anything from going to that new movie you've all been planning to see, to having a "milkshakes and manicures" get-together. Once you're done, fold up all the slips and put them in the jar. Seal the jar and put it somewhere safe. When everyone returns from their vacations, take turns picking slips of paper and letting the jar tell you what to do!

SECRET SURPRISES

Secretly slip little notes or stickers into your friend's suitcase or duffel bag before she leaves. You can even tuck some tiny messages into the pockets of her shorts or makeup bag. Hide them in any little secret spot you can find. Imagine her delight when she finds a surprise "hello" from you while she's away!

SUMMER SURVIVAL SOLUTIONS

Whether you're wondering how to survive
without your best friend for the summer or feeling
homesick at camp, here are some timely tips!

Best Friendless for the Summer

*My best friend is going to be
traveling with her family all
summer long. I'll be stuck here
at home all by myself. What
am I going to do?*

Your best friend may be going
on an adventure without you,
but that doesn't mean you can't
have a great summer, too! You
don't have to travel far and wide
to have an exciting time. There's
tons to do just outside your door.
Sign up for day camp, take
swimming lessons
at the public
pool, or get into
a new hobby or
sport at your local
community center
or Y. You'll have
tons of fun *and*
make new friends

at the same time. And when your
friend gets back from her travels,
you'll *both* have awesome tales
to tell! (Check out pages 8-10 for
more ideas on summer fun.)

Homesick Camper

*I was really looking forward to
camp, but now that I'm here, I
want to go home. The bunk beds
are uncomfortable, and I miss
my bedroom, my cat–and being
home! My best friend is here with
me but I don't think I can stay.*

Sounds like you're feeling the
same way Gwen did when she
first got to camp, even though
her best friend, Reese, was with
her. It's totally normal to be
homesick when
you're away. Even
though your best
friend is there
with you, trying

something new always takes
time to get used to. Once you've
spent several nights there, you're
likely to find that you miss home
less and less. And when you
start having a good time,
summer will fly right by!

SUM-SUM-SUMMERTIME FUN

Home for the summer?
Think there's nothing to do?
You can make exciting things happen.
Here are a few ways:

Get Sporty

Find a sport that you've never played before and sign up for it! A new sport can be anything from horseback riding to inner tubing to hiking. But as long as it's, well, new to you, it's a go. So if you've never tried swimming, beach volleyball, or skateboarding, give it a try! Check out your local community center or Y and see what they offer. If you come across something that you've never heard of or tried before and it sounds like fun, why not sign up?!

Hunt for Summer

Plan a summer scavenger hunt. Put summertime stuff on the list, like: a dandelion, watermelon seeds, a beach towel, a bottle of sunscreen, and a beach ball. Break up into teams and race to see which team collects all the things on the list first.

Go Wild

Go to the zoo, animal park, or nature preserve to view life on the wild side. Watch polar bears dive and play, let the monkeys entertain you with their funny faces, or go for a ride on an elephant or camel. If you feel like getting really close, go to a petting zoo where you can feed and pet your furry friends, or sign up to feed the dolphins!

Hit the Beach

Grab your sunglasses and sunscreen and head to the beach. Play paddleball, go boogie boarding, hop waves, or make a sand castle.

Open Shop

Organize a juice sparkler stand with some of your pals. You'll soak up the sun and make some spending cash, too! How do you make juice sparklers? Take some fruit juice and add a splash of club soda or ginger ale. Don't forget the ice! Here are some cool combos:

* **Ginger Ale Sparkler:** Pour 16 ounces of orange juice and 8 ounces of apple juice into a pitcher full of ice. Add 6 ounces of ginger ale, and stir it all up.

* **Grape Sparkler:** Mix 16 ounces of grape juice with 8 ounces of apple juice in a pitcher full of ice. Add 6 ounces of club soda and serve with a smile!

* **Sparkling Sunrise:** Pour 16 ounces of orange juice and 8 ounces of cranberry juice into a pitcher full of ice. Don't stir. Just add 6 ounces of club soda and watch the sunrise!

Dress up Your Wheels

Decorate your bike by putting colorful streamers or pretty ribbons through the spokes. Go cruising down the block and watch the streamers or ribbons wave in the wind!

Go Beach-Ball Bowling

Grab a beach ball and ten empty 2-liter bottles. Put some rocks or a little bit of dirt in each bottle to weigh them down. Set up the bottles like bowling pins and stand about ten feet back. Send your beach ball toward the bottles and see how many you can knock down!

Get Wet

Beat the summer heat by inviting your friends over for a day of water games. Load up the water guns, turn on the sprinkler, fill up those water balloons, and prepare to get wet! Looking for a few water games to try? Here are a couple:

✳**Water Balloon Toss:** Stand across from your partner and toss a water balloon back and forth. Here's the snag: You both take a step *back* after you make each catch. How far can you go before busting the balloon?

✳**Sprinkler Freeze–Dance:** Put on your bathing suits, turn on the tunes and sprinkler, and start boogying. One person controls the sprinkler and, when she turns it off, everyone has to freeze. First person to move is out!

Chalk It Up

Grab some sidewalk chalk and hit the pavement. Play hopscotch or tic-tac-toe, or get artistic and draw pictures on the sidewalk. Itching to get the word out? Write messages for your friends, family, or neighbors to see when they walk by.

Sleep Under the Stars

Put a tent up in the backyard and spend the night like a camper. Pretend that you're in the woods and nowhere near your house. That means no midnight runs to the fridge! Of course, you *could* always load up ahead of time....

Grow Something

Plant sunflower seeds and watch them grow into big smiling flowers as tall as you!

Dazzling SUMMER Duds

Get in touch with your inner Oki and re-design your sunglasses to let your sense of style come shining through.

Cool Shades

Get a plain pair of sunglasses and funk-ify them with this colorful beaded strap.

What You Need:

* Sunglasses
* 1 yard of silk cord
* Glue
* Beads

What You Do:

1. Tie one end of the silk cord onto the sunglasses—where the hinge is. Add a little dab of glue to keep the cord in place.

2. Start beading! Add beads onto the cord until it's long enough to fit comfortably around your neck.

3. Tie the other end of the cord to the other side of your sunglasses, and add a dab of glue to hold it in place. Let the glue dry before you use your new strap.

Don't Stop at the Strap

Add more pizzazz to your sunglasses. Cut shapes out of craft foam and glue them to the corners of the frames, or glue some little rhinestones on for sparkle. Feel like personalizing them even more? Get some small letter decals and add your initials, or write a message like: "Fun in the sun!" down the arms of your shades.

POPSICLE PARTY

What better way to have fun in the sun than with Popsicles all summer long!

POP-POP POPSICLE

What You Do:

What You Need:
- Paper cups
- Popsicle sticks
- Fruit juice
- Aluminum foil

Pour juice into a paper cup until it's about three-quarters full.

Cover the top of each cup with aluminum foil.

Push a Popsicle stick through the middle of the foil. (Use a piece of transparent tape to help keep it in place if it wiggles.)

Pop the cup in the freezer.

When your pop is frozen, take the foil off the top and peel off the paper cup. Now get ready to start lickin'!

RAINBOW POPS

What You Do:

Pick out three juice flavors for your rainbow pops. Try grape, cherry, and orange. How about cranberry or apple? Anything goes! Pick out your first flavor and fill the cup one-quarter of the way full.

Cover the cup with foil, pop the Popsicle stick through the center of the foil, and freeze.

Once that layer is frozen, add a second flavor. Pour enough to fill the cup halfway, and freeze again. Last layer time!

Add your third layer by pouring enough juice to fill three-quarters of the cup, and freeze one last time. Peel off the paper cups, and check out the pretty stripes.

CREAMY ORANGE POPS

What You Do:

1. Fill a paper cup three-quarters of the way with orange juice.

2. Add a spoonful of vanilla yogurt—but don't stir.

3. Cover with foil, poke in the Popsicle stick, and freeze. Creamy and icy at the same time!

FRUITY SURPRISE POPS

What You Do:

1. Fill a paper cup halfway with the fruit juice of your choice.

2. Now add some of your favorite fruit. Try a few banana slices, a few strawberry slices, or a couple of grapes.

3. Cover with foil and push the Popsicle stick through the center.

4. Once frozen, take the cup out and add more juice to fill the cup three-quarters of the way full. Cover and freeze. Enjoy while you look for your fruity surprise!

Tip: Use white grape juice for a see-through fruity pop!

POPSICLE-STICK PICTURE FRAMES

Need an excuse to eat lots of Popsicles? Use the sticks to make a cool picture frame for your friend. Add a photo of the two of you.

What You Need:
- Popsicle sticks
- Cardboard or posterboard
- Glue
- Photo

What You Do:

1. Cut posterboard or cardboard into a 3½ x 3½-inch square.

2. Squeeze a strip of glue along the left and right sides of the cardboard, and press a Popsicle stick onto each side. Glue two more Popsicle sticks, one each, across the top and bottom of the frame.

3. Glue another stick to the back of the frame so that it has a handle like a Popsicle.

4. Decorate the frame with paint, or use markers to write a message like "Best Friends Forever."

5. Once the glue has dried, add a photo of you and your friend.

French Baguette Pizza

Just like the Groovy Girls do at their *Bon Voyage* sleepover, you can make French baguette pizzas at your next get-together. *Ooh-la-la!*

What You Need:

- Pizza sauce
- Olive oil
- Shredded mozzarella cheese
- Baguette
- Aluminum foil
- Cookie sheet
- Knife
- Spoon
- Toppings like: pepperoni, green or red peppers, tomatoes, mushrooms, Parmesan cheese

What You Do:

1. Ask an adult to preheat the oven to 350 degrees.

2. Cover a cookie sheet with aluminum foil.

3. Split a baguette down its length, so you have two halves.

4. Cut each piece as big as you want each pizza to be—6 to 8 inches is a good size.

5. Drizzle a little bit of olive oil on top of each bread slice.

6. Spoon pizza sauce onto each slice and spread it around evenly.

7. Add shredded mozzarella cheese to each slice and let everyone add any toppings they want.

8. Place the pizzas on top of the foil-covered cookie sheet.

9. With a grown-up's help, pop the tray into the oven, and let the pizza bake until the cheese is melted (10-15 minutes).

10. *Voila*! Pizza, French style!

Yummy Pizza Combos:

Go Veggie:

Make an all-vegetable pizza by adding toppings like sliced tomatoes, mushrooms, green or red peppers, cooked spinach, or broccoli bits.

Extra Cheese-y:

If you're a cheese lover, mix up a blend of cheeses like shredded mozzarella, cheddar, Monterey Jack, and Parmesan. Cheeserific!

Create your own Groovy Girls character online at groovygirls.com

Gwen

Keeea

U'Ryan

Vanessa

Yvette

Groovy Girls®